I0526794

For my little sausages: Noah, Milo, Zen and Lotus
and for my mother Katharyn
and my sister Nefeterius- T.P.

For Pietro and my family - N.G.P.

www.theenglishschoolhouse.com

Text copyright © 2020 by Tamara Pizzoli
Pictures copyright © 2020 by Anna Angrick
All rights reserved.
This book or any portion thereof may not be reproduced or used in any manner what-
soever without the express written permission of the author except for the use of
brief quotations in a book review. This is a work of fiction. Names, characters, places,
and incidents are a product of the author's imagination. Any resemblance to actual
persons, events, or locales is entirely coincidental. The following high art paintings
featured in this book: Madonna and child, Cleopatra, Scheherazade, Aida I, Turandot,
Napoleone, Il Uomo Nero, The Pied Piper, Red Riding Hood and Venus appear courtesy
of Elena Tommasi Ferroni.
ISBN: 978-0-9992108-3-3

PIZZA PICASSO

Written by Tamara Pizzoli and Noah Giuliano Pizzoli
Illustrated by Anna Angrick

THE ENGLISH SCHOOL HOUSE

LA PIZZERIA
PIZZOLI
LA PIZZERIA PIZZOLI
DOC €11,00
PORCINA €11,00
CARCIOFINA €11,00
SICILIANA €11,00
FIOCCO €11,00
LASAGNA €11,00
ROMANA €11,00
BUFALINA €11,00
SAPORITA €11,00
NAPOLI €11,00
KOPÒ €11,00
CROCCO €11,00
CHEF €11,00
PARIGINA €11,00
GUSTOSA €11,00
MIMOSA €11,00
SEMPLICE €11,00
TONNARA €11,00
DIAVOLA €11,00
FILETTO €11,00
ORTOLANA €11,00
MARINARA €11,00

La Pizzeria Pizzoli had been in the
Pizzoli family for a long, long time.
And by a long, long time, we're talking
centuries... two of them to be exact.

Anything of quality that's been around a long time is bound to attract attention, and that was certainly the case with La Pizzeria Pizzoli. People came from all over the world to the center of Rome, Italy to savor just a slice. The estimated waiting time to reserve a table for dinner was over three months long.

There were hundreds, maybe even thousands of pizzerias in Rome, but none quite like La Pizzeria Pizzoli. For each and every year the pizzeria had been open for business, it had been owned and operated by a member of the family.

Well, Mr. President, La Pizzeria Pizzoli is more than a restaurant. It's our family's legacy.

Training for the family business began quite early. Starting in first grade, every Pizzoli helped out in the restaurant after school with the full understanding that their professional futures awaited within the walls of the eatery. Sebastian Pizzoli, age nine, was no exception.

In just three years of heading into the pizzeria after school, Sebastian had learned a great deal about what it takes to own a successful business.

"Do everything with love and tradition, Sebastian," his grandfather Nonno Ismaele would tell him. "It doesn't matter if you're sweeping the floor, kneading the dough, or counting the cash, every action needs care and love."

Like the Pizzolis who came
before him, Sebastian had
accepted the idea of his future as
owner of the family's business,
until one day his fourth grade
class took a field trip to an art
exhibition at a museum
featuring the work of the late,
great artist Pablo Picasso.

Sebastian was, in a word, floored. He had
never seen such incredible works of art.
He felt mesmerized, moved and speechless.
At that very moment, Sebastian knew his
calling was not to spend his days and nights
preparing pizzas at La Pizzeria Pizzoli.
His calling was art.

EXIT

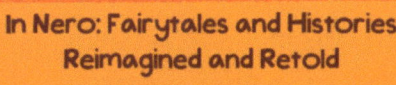

In Nero: Fairytales and Histories
Reimagined and Retold
Art by Elena Tommasi Ferroni
Curated by Tamara Pizzoli

Sebastian spent the next few weeks delving into the world of artistic genius and creativity. He went to museums and exhibitions after school with his parents. At his school library, he checked out literature on the artistic greats.

Amongst his favorite artists were Frida Kahlo, Jean Michel Basquiat, Tamara Madden, Andy Warhol, and the entire Tommasi Ferroni family.

But Nonno Ismaele was beginning to complain about his grandson's scarcity around the pizzeria. "I need more help around here!" he lamented to his son, Sebastian's father. "Sebastian's never around anymore!"

That night, Sebastian's parents had a heart to heart with their son. "We understand your passion for art, sweetie," his mother began, "but Nonno Ismaele really needs you at La Pizzeria Pizzoli." "Yes," Sebastian's dad chimed in, "the truth is, sometimes you have to make sacrifices to ensure the wellbeing of the family."

His father slid a box across the table toward Sebastian. Inside there were photos, trinkets and whatnots from his father's youth.
"I wanted to be a photographer, Sebastian, but the fact was the family business needed me more."
Sebastian nodded to show he understood.

The next day after school, he marched right over to La Pizzeria Pizzoli without making any stops."
"Ecco! Il mio nipote preferito!" his grandfather exclaimed with a clap of his hands. "There's my favorite grandson!"

Sebastian grinned, washed his hands, and grabbed an apron."
"I want kitchen duty today," Sebastian said assuredly. "
"Bravo!" his grandfather replied. "Vai in cucina!""

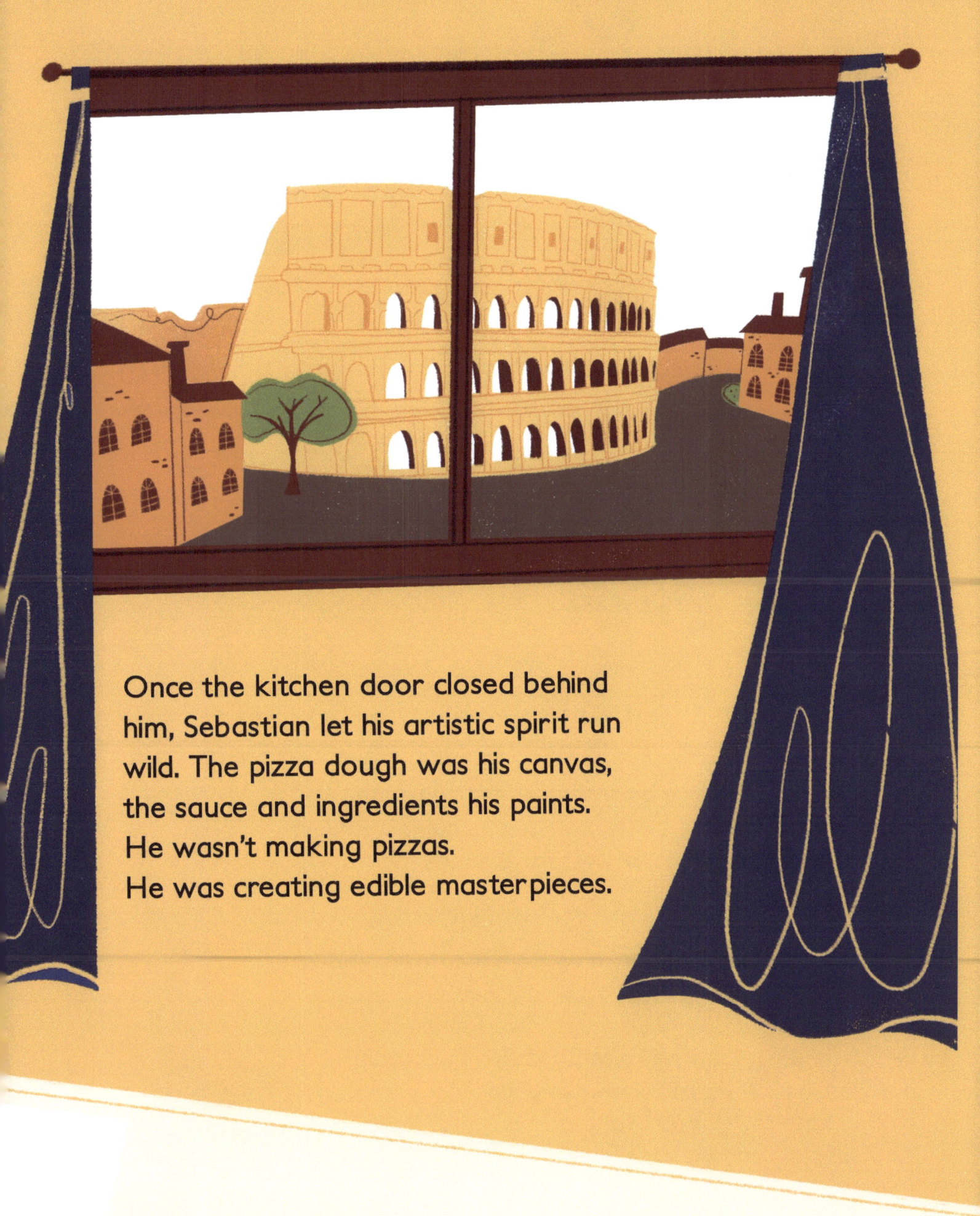

Once the kitchen door closed behind
him, Sebastian let his artistic spirit run
wild. The pizza dough was his canvas,
the sauce and ingredients his paints.
He wasn't making pizzas.
He was creating edible masterpieces.

He constructed a large portrait of Frida Kahlo with mozzarella, olive slices, chives, and green onions with cherry tomatoes and cauliflower for the table of vegetarians.

Next up was Sebastian's take on "La Gioconda" utilizing sliced hot dogs, olives, and provolone cheese.

By the time his "Untitled" piece, heavily influenced by Basquiat, hit the serving floor, the undeniable shrieks of Nonno Ismaele's disapproval could be heard down the block and around the corner.

Nonno Ismaele burst into the kitchen and headed directly for his grandson. "No no no no no no no, Sebastian! Assolutamente NO! Per favore! How many times do I have to tell you? Love and tradition, amore e tradizione! What did you just send out just now, eh? What was that mess? You're making chaos on the pizzas, Sebastian! The people don't come to La Pizzeria Pizzoli for innovation. They come for..."

Nonno Ismaele was interrupted mid-rant by a grand commotion. It was coming from the dining area."

Sebastian had to help Nonno Ismaele pick his jaw up off the floor. Soon after, the pizza piece was purchased by an art buyer from The Nef Gallery for 40,000 euro. She paid in two seconds with a swipe of her credit card and exited the pizzeria with her pizza in hand.

Nonno Ismaele was something Sebastian had never seen him be before...speechless. La Pizzeria Pizzoli had made more money in two minutes than it normally would in two months. Sebastian patted his grandfather on the back before offering the truth in four words:
"See, change is good.'"
Nonno Ismaele smiled and agreed.

UNTITLED
by Sebastian Pizzoli

€1,000,000.52

The next week Nonno Ismaele and Sebastian accepted an invitation to view Sebastian's pizza art piece "Untitled" on display at The Nef Gallery. They both nearly dropped the complimentary prosecco and juice they were given at the door once they noticed a tiny red dot just to the right of the pizza indicated it had already been acquired from the gallery by a private collector for €1,000,000.52.

www.ingramcontent.com/pod-product-compliance
Lightning Source LLC
Chambersburg PA
CBHW041546240626
47164CB00003B/142